Goodnight, Little One, Goodnight!

Written by
Marie Anna Laubert

Illustrated by
Justo Borrero

To the Readers
with love

This book belongs to:

The end of a busy day has come;
the sun is sinking deep.
It's time for little eyes to close,
for little children to sleep.

The birds nestle quietly in the trees
to rest for the day ahead,
and for little ones in their houses,
it's time to get ready for bed...

to put aside their toys and games
until another day,
to wash off all the dust and dirt
that gathered during play,

to brush their teeth
until each one is fully cleaned and white,
and put on soft pajamas.
It's time to say, "Goodnight!"

"Time for bed!" calls Mama Bear
when supper time is past.
"I'm not sleepy!" yawns Teddy,
but he does as Mama asks.

So it's into the tub for a vigorous scrub
as he's soaped from head to paw,
then into clean pajamas,
then to brush each tooth in his little bear jaw!

Then comes Teddy's favorite part:
Daddy carries him upstairs
and reads his favorite story... again!
"Goldilocks and the Three Bears."

Daddy helps Teddy say his prayers,
and as he turns out the light,
he smiles at Teddy and whispers,
"Goodnight, little Teddy, goodnight!"

It's time for bed at Elin's,
but Mama hasn't called yet.
Elin hoped Mama wouldn't remember,
but elephants never forget.

She has already filled Miss Elin's bath
and calls her to the tub
to soap from ears to trunk to feet…
an all-out elephant scrub!

Elin pulls on soft pajamas
and carefully brushes her teeth.
Then Mama helps her finish
where Elin couldn't reach.

Mama reads a bedtime story
and then hugs Elin tight.
Then, quietly, Mama whispers,
"Goodnight, little Elin, goodnight!"

Around the corner at Liam's house,
it's time to get ready for bed.
But Liam, future King of the Jungle,
would rather be ruling instead!

"You'll rule in your own, soapy bathtub,"
says Dad to his little King,
"and with clean pajamas and royal robe...
why, you can rule most anything!"

"I'm the jungle king!" roars Liam
after he's bathed and dressed.
He brushes his teeth to sparkling white,
then roars with even greater zest!

Then Daddy tucks Liam into bed
and prays for his heart's delight,
then whispers a bedtime story that ends:
"Goodnight, little Liam, goodnight!"

All through the house dances Giana Giraffe
in a magical world all her own,
until to her bath Grandma calls her,
in her sweet, familiar tone.

Giana whirls and twirls right into the tub
to wash the dirt away.
She lathers and rubs 'til the only spots left
are those that will always stay.

gianna

After donning her striped pajamas
and brushing her teeth with care,
Giana kneels by her bed with Grandma
to recite her evening prayer.

Then Grandma reads a fairytale
full of fantasy, fancy, and flight,
but when Giana drifts off, Grandma whispers,
"Goodnight, little Giana, goodnight!"

It's bath time for Hirro Hippo,
but Hirro is half asleep.
"I'm just too tired," yawns Hirro,
"I'd rather be counting sheep."

But Grandpa Hippo does not agree,
and into the tub Hirro goes
to soak in the warm bathwater,
submerged all the way to his nose.

He sits in the draining bathtub
until every drop is gone.
Then Grandpa helps him brush his teeth
and pull Hippohero pajamas on.

He gently tucks Hirro into bed
between fresh sheets of white
and whispers the teeniest story of all…
"Goodnight, little Hirro, goodnight!"

At Nickie's house it's bedtime,
or Mama Monkey says so.
Nickie's dancing, leaping, prancing...
wide awake: "Do I have to go?"

But Mama snatches Nickie up.
"We've reached the end of our day.
Let's brush your teeth and get your bath
so we can read, okay?"

In no time flat, Nickie's bathed and dry
and dressed in her princess gown.
She brushes her teeth and leaps into bed.
"Look, Mommy, I'm lying down!"

Mom brings a story, like every night,
kisses Nickie's cheeks, both left and right,
but she doesn't finish her story, quite.
"Goodnight, little Mommy, goodnight!"

A bright moon is glowing
like a giant lantern in the sky.
A million stars are dancing,
winking down at you from up on high.

The sun is waiting patiently
to rise and shine without delay.
And children should be sleeping,
dreaming of another day!

Teddy is sleeping, Elin is sleeping,
Giana is sleeping, too.
Liam is roaring into his dreams,
Jungle King the whole night through.

Even Hirro's sheep have gone to sleep,
And Nickie's eyes are closed,
Mommy got up and went to bed,
stirring shortly after she dozed.

If you've taken up your toothbrush
and cleaned your teeth, just so,
if you've had your bath,
and now you're fresh and clean from head to toe,

and you're in your soft pajamas,
why, you've got everything right!
So, close your eyes and get off to sleep!

Goodnight!

Goodnight!

Goodnight!

Thank you for choosing this book!

I hope you enjoyed it. I would like to know what you think about this book.

Your feedbacks help me create more awesome stories for you.

Looking forward to your comments, opinions, and suggestions.

Printed in Great Britain
by Amazon

31741906R00023